Usborne First Experiences

Anne Civardi
Edited by Michelle Bates
Illustrated by Stephen Cartwright
Cover design by Amanda Barlow

Medical adviser: Catherine Sims BSc; MBBS and Dr Lance King

Contents :

There is a little yellow duck hiding on every double page. Can you find it?

First published in 2001 by Usborne Publishing Ltd, Usborne House, 83-85 Saffron Hill, London EC1N 8RT, England
Copyright © 2001, 2000, 1992 Usborne Publishing Ltd.
First published in America in 2001.
The name Usborne and the device ⊕ are Trade Marks of Usborne Publishing Ltd.

Going to school

This is the Peach family.

Mrs. Peach

Mr. Peach

Polly
Peach

Pong
the
kitten

Percy
Peach

Sidney
the gerbil

Ping
the other kitten

Dusty the cat

Percy and Polly are twins. Tomorrow they are going to school for
the first time.

This is where the Peaches live.

They live above the Marsh family. Millie Marsh is going to the same school as the twins.

Mr. and Mrs. Peach wake Percy and Polly.

It is 8 o'clock in the morning. It is time for them to get ready
for school. Percy and Polly get up and get dressed.

They have their breakfast.

Then the twins put on their shoes and coats. Millie is ready to
go to school with them.

They all go to school.

At first, Polly is a little shy. Mrs. Todd, the teacher, says that Mrs. Peach can stay with her for a while.

Mr. Peach hangs Percy's coat on his own special hook. He has to take Percy's pet gerbil, Sidney, back home with him.

Percy and Polly join their class.

There are lots of things to do at school such as painting, drawing, reading and dressing-up.

Some children make things out of paper, and others make things with clay. What are Percy and Polly doing?

They have fun making things.

Two of the teachers help them make tiny washing lines full of clothes to take home.

It's time for singing.

Miss Dot, the music teacher, teaches them lots of different songs.
She also teaches them how to play lots of instruments.

Now it's time for a break.

At 11 o'clock, everyone has a drink and something to eat.
Percy and Polly are both very thirsty.

It's story time.

Mrs. Todd tells the children a story about a big tiger named
Stripes. What is Percy up to now?

The children go out to the playground.

There are lots of things to play with outside. There are tractors and hoops, and bicycles and balls.

Polly loves going down the slide. Percy likes to play in the sand. But Millie has found something else to play with.

It's time for Percy and Polly to go home.

They have had a happy day at school and so has Millie. They have made lots of new friends.

Going to the doctor

This is the Jay family.

Mrs. Jay

Mr. Jay

Jack Jay

Jenny Jay

Joey Jay

Nod

Rory

Jenny has woken up with a bad cough and Jack has hurt his arm.
They must go and see the doctor.

Mrs. Jay phones the doctor.

She makes an appointment while Mr. Jay helps Jack get dressed.
"Ow," shouts Jack, "watch my arm, Dad."

The Jays go to see the doctor.

Mrs. Jay takes Jack, Jenny and Joey to see Doctor Woody. "We've got an appointment at 2 o'clock," she tells the receptionist.

The receptionist checks her book.

"Yes, it's for Jack and Jenny, isn't it?" she says. "And for Joey too," Mrs. Jay reminds her. "He needs to have his immunization."

The Jays sit in the waiting room.

There are lots of people waiting to see the doctor. Mrs. Jay reads
a book to Jenny. Jack and Joey want to play.

Now it is the Jays' turn.

Doctor Woody calls their name. "Who shall I see first?" she says.
"Me," says Jack, holding out his arm.

Doctor Woody examines Jack.

She looks at his sore arm. "It's not broken," she says, "but you do have a sprained wrist, Jack."

Doctor Woody puts Jack's arm in a sling.

"Just wear this for a few days," Doctor Woody tells him. "It will feel better soon."

Doctor Woody checks Jenny.

She takes her temperature with a thermometer. Then she looks down Jenny's throat. "It's very red," she says.

Then she examines Jenny's ears with an auroscope. "Your ears are fine," she tells Jenny.

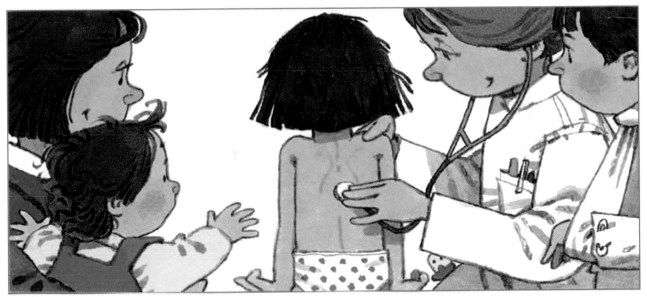

Doctor Woody listens to Jenny's breathing with a stethoscope. "Breathe in and out deeply," she says.

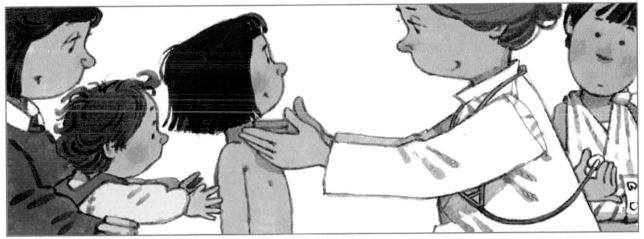

She feels Jenny's neck to see if her glands are swollen. "You have a slight chest infection," she says.

Jenny needs some medicine.

Doctor Woody prints a prescription for Jenny from her computer.
Then she sits down at her desk and signs it.

Now it is Joey's turn.

Doctor Woody gives Joey his immunization. It only hurts a little.

She also gives Joey some drops so that he won't get polio. Then she says goodbye to the Jays.

The Jays pick up Jenny's prescription.

Mrs. Jay stops at the pharmacy. She gives the pharmacist the prescription and he gives her some medicine.

At home, Mrs. Jay puts Jenny to bed.

Mrs. Jay tucks Jenny in and gives her a spoonful of medicine.
"You'll be better soon," she says.

That evening, Mr. Jay comes home from work.

"Hello everyone," he says. "How are you all?" Jack jumps to his feet.
"Joey's all right, and Jenny's in bed," he says. "But look at my sling!"

Moving house

This is the Spark family.

Mr. Spark

Mrs. Spark

Sam Spark

Peter

Sophie Spark

Patch

Sam is seven and Sophie is five. They are moving into a new house very soon.

This is the Sparks' old house.

They have sold it to Mr. and Mrs. Potts. The Potts have come today to measure the rooms.

The Sparks go to see their new house.

The house is being painted before the Sparks move in. Mr. Spark
makes friends with the people who live next door.

Two men from Cosy Carpets arrive to put new carpets down in some of the rooms.

The Sparks pack up their old house.

It takes many days for Mr. and Mrs. Spark to sort out all of their things. Packing is hard work.

Sam makes sure that all of his things are packed too. But Sophie
would rather play.

The Sparks move.

Early in the morning, a big truck arrives to take the Sparks' furniture to their new home.

Bess

Bill, the driver, and Frank and Bess, his helpers, load everything
into the big truck. Then they drive it to the new house.

Everyone helps unload the truck.

Bill shows Sam and Sophie the inside of the truck. Then they all start to take the things into the new house.

They take things inside.

Bill, Frank and Bess carry the heavy furniture into the house. Mrs. Spark shows them where to put everything.

This is Sophie's new bedroom.

Dad helps Sophie to get it ready. He puts up the curtains. Sophie is very excited about having a new room.

Sam has his own room too.

Sam likes the new house. Now he does not have to share a room with Sophie. Mrs. Spark helps him unpack.

The Sparks meet the people from next door.

In the afternoon the Sparks go for a walk down their street. There are lots of people to meet.

Mrs. Tobbit

Sophie and Sam will have some new friends to play with. Mrs. Tobbit from next door gives Mr. Spark a big cake to welcome them.

The Sparks go to bed.

Mr. and Mrs. Spark, Sophie and Sam are very tired after the move.
They fall fast asleep in their new home.

The new baby

This is the Bunn family.

Mrs. Bunn

Mr. Bunn

Lucy
Bunn

Spock

Tom
Bunn

Bertie

Lucy is five and Tom is three. Mrs. Bunn is going to have a baby soon.

Granny and Grandpa come to stay.

They are going to look after Lucy and Tom when Mrs. Bunn is in the hospital. Lucy and Tom are excited to see them.

The Bunns get ready for the new baby.

There is a lot to do before the baby is born. Mr. and Mrs. Bunn decorate the baby's bedroom.

Lucy and Tom help too. Mrs. Bunn paints the bed for the baby to sleep in. Lucy uses the baby's bath to wash her doll.

Mrs. Bunn feels the baby coming.

Mrs. Bunn wakes up in the middle of the night. She thinks that the baby will be born very soon.

Everyone wakes up.

Mr. Bunn gets ready to take her to the hospital while Grandpa phones to say that they are on their way.

The baby is born.

It is a little girl. Mr. and Mrs. Bunn are very happy. They are going to name her Susie.

Nurse Cherry weighs Susie to see how heavy she is, and measures her to see how long she is.

Susie is wrapped in a blanket to keep her warm. She has a name tag on her tiny wrist so she doesn't get mixed up with other babies.

As soon as Dad gets home, he tells Lucy and Tom all about their baby sister, Susie. They can't wait to see her.

They visit Susie.

The next day, Mr. Bunn takes Lucy and Tom to the hospital.
They are very excited to see their mother and baby sister.

Mrs. Bunn is in a room with two other mothers. They have new babies too. One of the mothers has twins.

The next day, Mrs. Bunn and Susie come home.

Mr. Bunn picks them up from the hospital. Everyone is excited and wants to hold the baby.

Susie goes to bed.

Susie is very sleepy. Mrs. Bunn is tired too. She will need a lot of help from Lucy, Tom and Mr. Bunn.

Mrs. Bunn feeds Susie.

When Susie is hungry, Mrs. Bunn feeds her with milk. Susie will need to be fed many times each day.

Susie has a bath.

Now it is time for Susie's bath. Mr. Bunn is very careful. Lucy helps her Dad wash and dry Susie.

The Bunn family goes out.

Mr. and Mrs. Bunn, Lucy and Tom take Susie for a walk. They are all very excited about the new baby.